The Pride Street Crew

13

Now I Know
How It Feels

Mike Wilson

Published in association with
The Basic Skills Agency

Hodder & Stoughton

Acknowledgements
Cover: Jim Eldridge
Illustrations: Jim Eldridge

Orders; please contact Bookpoint Ltd, 39 Milton Park, Abingdon, Oxon OX14 4TD. Telephone: (44) 01235 400414, Fax: (44) 01235 400454. Lines are open from 9.00–6.00, Monday to Saturday, with a 24 hour message answering service. Email address: orders@bookpoint.co.uk

British Library Cataloguing in Publication Data
A catalogue record for this title is available from the British Library

ISBN 0 340 776374

First published 2000
Impression number 10 9 8 7 6 5 4 3 2 1
Year   2005 2004 2003 2002 2001 2000

Typeset by GreenGate Publishing Services, Tonbridge, Kent.
Printed in Great Britain for Hodder and Stoughton Educational, a division of Hodder Headline Plc, 338 Euston Road, London NW1 3BH, by Atheneum Press, Gateshead, Tyne & Wear

JOHN/ BONE

WESLEY/ TALL

LUKE/SKY

SIMON / CUSTARD

CARL / SPOT.

Wesley has a brother, right?
Tyrone.

He sells car hi-fi
in a shop in town.

Tyrone is crazy about his car.
He won't park it on the road.
Every night
he parks on the garden,
an inch from the house.
So no one can get in the car door.

I think it's crazy.
But Wesley says
that car is Tyrone's pride and joy.
He has to know it's safe.

Two nights ago,
Tyrone came out of work.
His car was gone.
No one saw it happen.
No one heard the alarm go off.

The police found the car today,
forty miles away.
It was a write-off.
The stereo was ripped out.
The windows were all smashed.
The wheels were gone.

Tyrone was gutted.
Wesley was gutted too.
He really felt for his brother.

I just could not see it.

'What's the problem?' I said.
'It's just a car.
He can get another one.'

'No,' said Wesley.
'It's more than that.
A car says something about you.
It's who you are.'

'That's sad, Wesley!' I said.
'It's just a metal box.
It gets you from A to B.'

'It wasn't you,' Wesley said,
'So you don't care.
If *you* lost something you cared about ...'

I just didn't see it.
Maybe I didn't want to see it.
I didn't think about Tyrone again
for a few weeks
and then it all came back to me.

When it happened to me,
I knew just how Tyrone felt.

The story started months ago.

I was working for Uncle Ray one day.
He asked me:

'Do you want a bike, Luke?
There's a man on the market
selling them cheap.
Why not go and check them out?'

When I got there,
it was love at first sight.

The man had lots of really cool bikes.
But they all cost a ton of money.
More than I could afford.

Then I saw this really cool one –
a Road Star Sport 550.
The man said it needed a bit of work.
That's why it was cheap.

I went back to Uncle Ray.
He said he'd give me a loan.
I could pay him back a bit at a time.

So I went back to the bike man
and gave him the cash.
I got a lock, a chain
and a set of lights.

It was my birthday in a few weeks.
I got Mum and Dad
to get me some new alloy wheels.
I had some money off my Gran.
I spent it on some No-shock forks.
Then I got myself a 9-speed gear wheel.

Then I let Mum get me a helmet.
Just to stop her worrying about me.

I went all over town on my new bike.
I went to school.
To Lizzy's.
To the market on Saturdays.

I started going on long rides on Sundays.
I'd do twenty miles,
or more.
I went off-road,
and came back caked with mud.

When I got home
I took everything apart.
I'd clean everything.
Then I put it all back together again.

It took hours.

I started hanging round bike shops,
looking at gear … .
I'd stand still on two wheels
for hours,
looking in the shop window … .

Dreaming of the perfect bike.

I paid Uncle Ray back
as soon as I could.
Then I started to save up
for some new hubs, with disk brakes.

Disk brakes were the latest thing.
Even Carl didn't have disk brakes.
I knew I'd be the only kid on Pride Street
– the only kid in the school –
with disk brakes.

I just couldn't wait.

It took me nearly six months,
and it nearly killed me.

But I did it.

In the end,
I had a bit of a loan from Mum
and a bit of a loan from Lizzy.
Just to help me out a bit.

At last, one Saturday,
I went down to Free Wheel,
the new bike shop in town.
I was getting a set
of Hi-Ten VX 20 disk brakes.

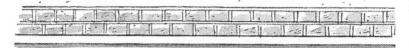

I chained my bike up outside,
and went in.
They knew me in here by now.
I came in all the time.
Normally I didn't spend any money
but I'd make up for that today!

The new brakes cost me over £120
but they'd be worth it.

I couldn't wait
to see the look on Carl's face
when he saw them.

I'd show the rest of the Crew
at school on Monday.
The best bike in the world!

I gave the man my money,
and he gave me the little box
with the VX 20s in.

I checked all the bits were there.
Then I stuck the box
in my bag.

I didn't stay and look round the shop
on my way out.
There was nothing else I wanted.
I just wanted to get home
and fit my new VX 20s.

Outside the shop,
I found a few pieces of my chain
lying on the ground.

It had been cut,
quick and neat,
by experts.

The best bike in the world
had gone.

If you have enjoyed reading about the Pride Street Crew, you may be interested in other books in the series.

It's Not the Winning
Carrot Rap
You Can't be a Kid For Ever
She Likes Me
No Turning Back
Child's Play
Damp Dog
Say It to My Face
Who Do You Love?
Let's Go Shopping
A Thousand Reasons
Make a Splash!
You're Never Alone With a Phone